It's A Jun E Day!!!

Written by Jay Caniel

Illustrated by Tiya Caniel Maynard

ISBN: **0692057862**
ISBN-13: **978-0692057865**

DEDICATION

To all the dreamers in this life.
To the universe up high.
To the territory that spreads wide.
To the unlimited capacity of happiness inside.
To smiles that make smiles.
To auras that make it pleasant to be alive.
To the visionaries who never lost sight.
To the strong,
The bold,
The ones who go the extra mile.
To the great intentions and all the people who subscribe.
To One Race and those of us against divide…

Thank you, from Little Brown Eyes

It's A Jun E Day!

Sunrise!!! It's morning time!

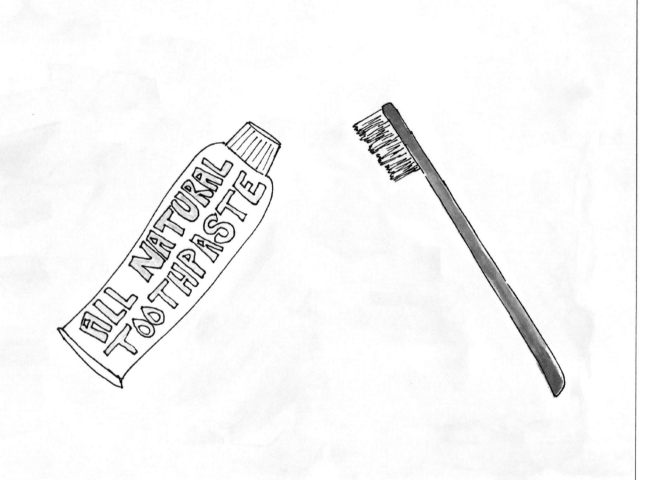

Mommy said, "Brush your teeth so they can stay white."

Breakfast on the table.
Yum! Yum!

Pancakes, fruit, fresh juice.
What a delight!

Time for school!

Learning makes me smile.

I love the glasses my teacher wear over her eyes.

I'm paying attention so I can get a prize.

I can count to 100 and I just turned five!

Yes!
It's recess, my favorite time!

Maybe we'll get to swing for a little while...

Or run around the playground like lions.

Oh how could I forget the feeling of going down the slide?!?!
Wheeeeeeeeeeeeeeeeee!!!!

It's a Jun E day!
And soon it will be snack time!

Can't wait to go home and dream tonight.

Maybe I'll be eat all my vegetables at dinner time.

Then I can bargain for 10 minutes of T.V. time...

I've been a good boy so Mommy just might comply.

Made in the USA
Columbia, SC
01 May 2018